STEAMPUNK

Robin Boyle lives in Sussex.

Steampunk

Robin Boyle

THE REAL PRESS
www.therealpress.co.uk

Published in 2017 by the Real Press.
www.therealpress.co.uk © Robin Boyle

The moral right of Robin Boyle to be identified as the author of this work has been asserted in accordance with the Copyright, Designs and Patents Acts of 1988

ISBN (print) 978-1912119691
ISBN (epub) 978-1912119684

I

As I looked out from the balcony on Deck 3, I realised how much I enjoyed flying. I enjoyed being the pilot, being a gunner, and even being an engineer. The wind against your face and knowing that a nice warm supper was waiting for me when I got to the barracks. That was enough to make me join the army.

I had been in the army for ten years now. I started when I was 15 and I am now 25. It was all that time and fighting that made me an officer. An officer and a captain of the Royal Icrises army. In fact, I was just coming back to home after a five-year campaign in North Trelinster. My superiors were calling it a strategic retreat but, judging by the mood everyone's in, I seriously doubt it.

The war had been raging for fifty years. This is the way it stood: Icrises vs. Trelinster, Trelinster vs. Balbar, and finally Everyone Hates Senetea. You see, Icrises, Trelinster, and Balbar are rebel factions, offcuts from Senetea. Now, Senetea is the main controlled faction that is not in rebellion and every single rebel faction despises them. But they can't show it as everyone knows that the army and aerships of Royal Senetea would be able to crush them in one strike. And every faction was too full of themselves to come together and wipe out Senetea. Oh, and if I said that out loud, I would have probably been killed. So you're lucky to catch me saying it.

Two hours later, we could see the docking area. "Rope cannons!" I shouted.

Rope fired out of the sides of the aership. People on the ground rushed to grasp them and we went slowly downwards.

"Cut balloon! Cut engine!" I shouted over the sound of the rushing air, as the ground became closer and closer.

The ship shuddered as it hit land. Wooden walkways fell down from the deck and 200 men rushed onto their home turf. The crew and I exited last, saying a few parting words to the landing crew.

"Tie her up in section 5, please."

"Sure thing, Boss."

A coach pulled up. "Corneal Laurence wishes to see you, sir," the coach driver said. Slowly, I stepped into the coach.

In five minutes, we approached the manor on the

gravel drive. It had been a hot day and the fountain made my mouth water. "Here we are, sir. Sinborn Manor."

As I stepped out of the coach, I looked up to the large three-storey house. Its splendour surprised me. Or maybe that was just because I had just spent five years in North Trelinster. "Hello, Captain," said Laurence. "Come in. We need a chat."

So I followed him inside, through the large corridor with 'famous' paintings on the wooden walls and then it to his office. It was a smallish room with a desk on one side and the door on the other. All around the room were scattered old pictures with mostly him featuring in them.

"Have a seat," he said, kindly. I relaxed at the softness of them. He poured a drink and passed one to me. I passed it back saying: "No, thanks. I don't drink."

"Oh," he replied, obviously taken back. "Right. You're a good officer, Sam. Really good. But you could be even better."

"How?" I said. "I would certainly like to be better."

"I am going to promote you. Captain to admiral. Officer to corneal. I can't say I was surprised. His manner said it all. "Thank you, sir!" I said gratefully; it had always been my ambition to make corneal.

"This brings me to my next announcement. Now you're a corneal, you are required to lead another campaign – so that is exactly what you're going to do. You'll be leading a campaign into North Trelinster again. We'll give you a few weeks to see your family and friends. All your belongings are on the aership now so there's no need the pack," said Corneal Laurence, in a orderly way.

"Now you're a smart boy," said Laurence. "You know the retreat out of Trelinster was a proper one. They simply had more men than us. Which is why, this time, were taking double the amount of men!"

II

In a few weeks, I was back on the *Flame Bringer* and was just flying over Lake Concan, when a message pigeon arrived with a radiogram. It was delivered by my first mate, Jim.

"Here you are, sir! Radiogram from RIAS *Speed Bringer.*"

I opened the radiogram with curiosity. It read as follows: *Start: Emergency STOP: Five Senetea cutters. STOP: Following hidden STOP: Requesting help. END.*

After reading it through several times, I went up the steps to the helm and ordered the boat forty-five degrees to the right. Then I yelled: "Ready battle stations! Cannons out!"

With that, I rushed down and ordered a signal to the fleet behind us to follow our lead. And then, five minutes later in the distance, I could see cannon fire and hear it too. "READY CANNONS! STAND BY TO FIRE!"

We pulled into range. "STANDBY TO FIRE!" I yelled, as all the ships on my line came one by one into line.

"FIRE!" Fire blasted from the sides of our ships. The *Speed Bringer*, having realised we had answered her SOS call, drew to broadside and fired. The noise of cannon fire echoed around us. Suddenly, two of the Senetea ships burst into flame and immediately fell from the sky, leaving only screaming, falling people behind them.

Another line of fire burst from our line. We had already lost three ships. But as soon as each were gone, another came to replace it. We were wasting time firing at them.

"Stand by to board the three remaining ships!" I shouted and, as if they had anticipated my move, the line moved forward still firing, but only the front cannons. Soon we drew into line with the remaining ships. Down the boarding board went.

With a "CHARGE!" from the men, we jumped onto their front line. I unholstered my gun, as did many others, and I took down a few before charging myself into the battle. My sword dashed around, cutting, slicing and stabbing, while my gun flashed taking down several before I was forced to reload.

As it would take a long time, I holstered my gun, using my sword instead. Jabbing and slashing, I got caught in a fight with the enemy ship's captain.

He skipped away for a moment and in a moment I had reloaded my gun, but was too preoccupied dodging his sword to use it. Then I saw my moment. Only taking a second to take my gun out of the holster, I pointed it at is head. In just a moment, a bullet was in his skull and he was on the floor. The rest of the crew surrendered promptly.

"Do we leave no prisoners?" Jim asked. I knew that I would let them go if possible but, if I did that, they would probably go screaming to their master that a fleet of airship was crossing into Trelinster. So my answer was a sorry one for the remaining crew. I looked away as swords were raised and brought down continually.

Ten minutes later, we were back on our way towards North Trelinster.

I immediately wrote in my logbook. *Attacked five Senetea cutters. RIAS Death, and RIAS Unbreakable sunk. Enemy ships Order and Vice sunk. Boarded ship. Fight. Battle won. All enemy sailors killed. Enemy ships Crow and Robin scuttled.*

After two more hours, we could see Trelinster. A small patrol team was on the border. Our order was to land, kill the patrol team and make a stealthy advance into Trelinster, killing all solders until we got to Castle Lokk where the real battle will commence. So I gave the order to land silently.

Quietly, the doors were dropped and slowly we approached the wooden wall that is the border to Trelinster. Slowly we placed the explosives at the bottom of the wall and set the fuse alight. Hurriedly, we ran back to the airship. The wall burst open with a boom and a flash. Rubble sprayed everywhere. Gunfire came through the hole and hit a few of our men.

Hurriedly, we returned fire, crawling through long grass creeping up on the small patrol. We dashed out of cover. The patrol was taken by surprise and drew their swords, blocking some of the attack and then slashing back at their attackers. I brought one down and shot an approaching solider.

The ambush was over soon and, after all the soldiers were off the airboats, we started to march. After about six hours of marching, the solders morale was falling, so I ordered a halt. We set up camp in an abandoned farmhouse. Tents were set up next to house and I set up a bed for myself. Soon, the murmuring from the men and the crackling from the fire had sent me to sleep.

I was woken in the early hours of the morning, by Jim. I got dressed and went to breakfast. Army rations. Soon we had packed up camp and were back on the road, the morale high. We took our second worst and most dangerous path: Death Alley. A small path two metres long and, on either side, we were surrounded by twenty metre high rocks. We were basically walking down a crevasse. And all crevasses are perfect for ambush.

We had walked for three hours and were well into the crevasse. People glanced up the high wall, looking for possible enemies.

Finally the men saw a light at the end of the tunnel. They started to run. I tried to stop them but it was no use. Fear had taken them. There was no stopping them. They were safe. Or so they thought.

The first men out fell down. Suddenly shock spread down the ranks and they started to back up. It was too late. About ten men jumped out of the rocks at the exit and shot at the fleeing men. The men turned and charged, as our clan was known for its barbarism. More men fell as we reached the exit and flung ourselves into attacking the front men. More fell.

I ducked under a rock and drew my gun. I shot a few over my makeshift cover. Then a couple more. Soon they realised how many of their men were falling dead. They looked in my direction and saw a gun poking out of the top of the rock, then they charged at me. I unsheathed my sword and ran at them. I cut down the first person as the second came for me. I plunged my sword into his gut and moved on to the next. I put a bullet in his head and ducked as his comrade's sword came at me. I kicked up and he went down.

I shouted: "Rally and charge at the front!" It was no use. We were so disorganised. I gathered what men I could and ran to the entrance. We charged as one and took them on. I took down four with my pistol then charged into the next with my sword. We had breached the wall.

"RUN!" I yelled and ran myself. We ran until we arrived at an old town that looked abandoned. We camped in one of the houses there. Losses had been bad. We had lost over a hundred men. A third of us had been killed. We went to bed and fell asleep, depressed.

In the morning, I had a large decision to make. Would we give up on our campaign or plough through it. My choice was clear. I ordered a full retreat.

The men did not take this that well. Even though they knew what I had to do. We could not hope to capture North Trelinster with only 200 men. We had to go home. We walked all day until we reached the place where we had slept the first night. We all settled in fast. After all the walking that day, we were ready for a large rest.

Early the next morning, there were sounds of people of talking in the camp. I came out of my tent and I was surprised by what I saw. A line of my warriors had formed a protective barrier in front of the camp. I pushed myself to the front and I was even more surprised. An organised line of Trelinster solders stood on the other side of the field. You could sense the fear in our ranks. One of my officers came up to me and saluted.

"We have been ambushed again, sir." Almost immediately after he said it, three horses emerged out of enemy lines. Dust rose up around them. They were carrying the white flag of parley. Our solders noticed that and opened our ranks. They rode right up to us. We growled. They dismounted and walked towards me, bodyguards on either side. "This is your last chance to surrender. You have five hours to get out of Trelinster. Then we attack," their corneal said.

"We won't back off!" I said. "Let us fight to the death. And make this land run with blood!" My men cheered.

"So be it. Your death day is today. Say your prayers!" He replied and mounted his horse. When he left, I went to the front of our line.

"Today, we face the Trelinster scum," I said. "We may not be victorious but at least our souls will be remembered!" I yelled into our lines. They cheered.

"So let's remember that we are sons of warriors!" I shouted. They cheered again. Our spears were raised into the air. "Form ranks. Let nobody through! Load guns and fire at my word!"

The enemy started to advance. "GUNS! AIM!" I shouted. The lines advanced further then they started to gather speed.

"FIRE!" The front line of men fell.

"CHARGE!" Our lines clashed into the enemy's. Blood sprayed. I charged and shot a few, then cut an attacking man in half. As I moved onto the next person the man next to me fell to the ground with a bullet in his head. I shot the man who had just done that and put my sword in his gut. A bullet rushed past me to hit Jim. He lay dying on the floor. I would have gone to help him, but two men charged at me. I shot one and dodged the sword that was coming towards me. Then I punched him in the jaw.

Blood came out of his mouth and I started to run towards Jim. A sword ripped through his lifeless body. I gasped. Just as I looked up a massive club came down on me.

I went out like a light.

III

I woke up feeling horrible. Everything was blurry. I was in an iron cage. Guards walked past me. They wore the sign of Trelinster. I sighed. My first worry was getting out. I looked down to where my sword should be. It was gone. So was my gun. I called out to one of the guards.

I had a plan. I could come up with plans very quickly. That was why the army had taken a liking to me. The guard ignored me. "Oi, Fat-Face!" I yelled.

He looked my way with a scowl on his face. "Do you what to get beaten up?" he asked in a confidential voice.

"If you can get your fat fingers through the bars, sure," I replied.

"You know, I think that Boss will forgive me. Just this one time." He said as he walked towards me. He drew the key and opened the cage. Immediately I swung into action and kicked him the stomach. He fell to the ground winded. Then he jumped into action and threw a punch at me. I dodged it easily and grabbed it. Then I pulled on his arm, throwing him to the other side of the cage.

"Thanks for these," I said, as I picked out the keys out of the lock and walked after locking him in. I was now in a stone corridor. I carefully made my way towards a wooden door and pushed it open. There were signs above it. I then saw the word ARMOURY. I decided to follow it, as my first objective was to get weapons to defend myself. I went along a stone walkway until some stairs. I went up them and was shocked by what I saw.

I had just walked onto a stone wall. The city surrounded me. I was in a fortress. Below me was a town with people walking around. There was a market place and lots of solders. This was definitely not the armoury. I made my way quietly down the stairs. There was a door. Finally, I had found what I was looking for. I made for the nearest bunch of weapons. I picked up a sword and put it in my sheath. Luckily that hadn't been taken away. Next, I got a pistol and 17 rounds of bullets.

I was ready now. I ran out of the room and made my way to the way to the walls. When on top of them, I ducked and carefully lowered rope down the side. But before I went down I made sure I did something that they would remember me by. I grabbed a torch from one of the battlements and threw it down into the town. Then I jumped, hoping that my rope would hold. I grabbed on and slowly slid my way down the wall.

At last, I reached the bottom. A nearby house was on fire. Soon it would spread to the houses around it. Screaming had started. Panic would soon spread though the whole town. I started to run towards an aership. There were two guards at the gates of the dock. I ducked and levelled my gun. I shot at one of them, taking him down. The next one waited a second, shocked that the person he was just talking to lay dead at his feet. His hesitation was his downfall, as I put bullet in his head.

I then ran swiftly into the dock and made my way to the smallest ship. Then, suddenly, the ship in front of me burst into flame. I looked across to see two men, one holding a bow. I drew my sword. Then two more men charged at me from behind the smaller boat. Before I could raise my gun to shoot, they both fell to the ground. They both had an arrow embedded in them. I looked up and saw the man lower his bow.

I was obviously not considered one of them. Cautiously I walked towards him. He lowered his bow. Then he raised his hand. "So good to see you, my friend!" He yelled across the dock.

He then started to run. I then realised it was my

second officer, Jak.

"Hi! You here as well?" I shouted back. Next to him, another solider ran. I recognised him from the front line of the battle.

"We should get into one of these aerships!" He said once he had arrived I nodded. "But we don't number enough to man them," I replied with worry.

"We shall pick one of the smaller vessels," he said. We clambered onto a small ship and he made his way to the steering wheel while the other man loosed the rigging. "Seems you started a pretty large fire back there," he said.

As we started to ascend, a patrol of five men walked into the docks and levelled their gun. As they started to shoot, I clambered into one of the smaller guns this ship had and shot back. Two men fell but the other three kept on shooting. More men arrived. "Get going!" I shouted over the roar of the wind and fire. I sniped a few more. Bullets whistled past me and hit the sail next to balloon. A hissing sound started as the air started to drain out of the ship.

I yelled. I jumped up to some spare cloth and stuck it over the hole and applied some glue. It stuck in moments and I was back to killing all the men on the ground. Anti-aircraft cannons roared into action. They were obviously not afraid of wrecking their own ship. When we had reached 1,500 feet, I looked below to see the massive fire that I had started. The town was made out of wood so the fire spread in seconds. People ran for their lives. I saw two ships ascending after us. I yelled out to Jak. "WE GOT COMPANY!" over the roar of the engine.

Almost immediately, their cannons fired. Both missed. We returned fire as more cannons joined the fire-fight. Soon we had reached the town wall. The fire had spread immensely. The noise of wooden houses crashing to the ground filled the air. The two ships that had been chasing us fired again. Luckily one of them missed but the other hit our hull, sending a rocking motion throughout the ship. I almost fell over but used the handrail to steady myself and push me back on my feet.

I ran over to the stairs leading to the lower deck and went down them. A metre-wide hole met me. I was shocked and called out to Jak: "THERE'S A MASSIVE HOLE IN OUR HULL!"

I ran over to the spare wood and plastered it over the hole. I then used a hammer to hammer it back in place. I then rushed up back to the gun and shot back. Our ship was tinny compared to theirs. Our only chance were to get one on either side. "Go into the middle of them!" I yelled.

"That's madness! We will be killed," Jak yelled back, preoccupied with steering the ship. He trusted me though, even though he thought it to be madness.

I could feel the ship turning towards the enemy. I shot my gun and saw it hit the other ship's hull. "YES!" I exclaimed. I reloaded and aimed my next shot. We were now pointing directly towards them. All we could do now was steer straight forwards. By getting inside the enemy, we could get all our guns to bear. The risk was that by getting inside them, they also had all their guns bearing on us.

We had soon entered the area between the boats and, the moment that happened, all hell broke lose. They launched their cannons at us and both hit us, one on the mast, one on the hull, not piercing the armour. I fired then reloaded as fast as I could. My shot hit the deck ripping through it. A man screamed then jumped overboard as a cannon ball ripped through him. The other ship fired their cannons, one missing but the other hitting the hull right where I had fixed it. I didn't bother this time.

We were now right next to the two ships. I drew my pistol and shot the man opposite me. He fell dead and the man next to him rushed over to take over the gun. I lined up my shot and fired. The cannon ripped through the ship and hit were they stored the gun powered. The ship exploded in a roar and flames burst from. One ship down. One to go.

Two more guns fired from the enemy ships. They

both hit the hull, one penetrating and one bouncing off, inches away from the magazine. The next shot and we were down. The mast had almost fallen, the hull had been penetrated twice and the magazine was dangerously open. Jak knew this as well and tried to turn the ship around, but it was too late.

Before we knew it, the enemy cannons were loaded again and were ready to fire. We knew this was our last moment. I sent a quick prayer up to the havens and waited for my death to come. Everything happened in a split-second. The sound of cannons being fired and everything roaring into flame on the other ship. As it slowly fell downwards, three massive ships came into view with the Icrises flag flying over their masts.

Jak and the man with him broke into cheers as the three ships roared into battle firing, all of their cannons, taking down the ship that had long chased us. The ship burst into flames, killing all that were in it in seconds. Cheers burst out of the newcomers as well. Soon the three ships sailed alongside us and threw boarding ropes for us to cross. I carefully made my way along the boarding line and jumped into the ship.

People greeted me. That surprised me. If anything, they should have shouted at me for failing to complete the campaign. No doubt that the Elders back in Icrises would want the entire note on what happened.

I was led down to the lower decks where a bed and food had been prepared for me. I didn't bother with the food, even though I was so hungry. I just fell asleep.

IV

In five hours, we had docked at the Icrises capital city, Kakuri. At the docks, small and large aerships were refuelling. Sailors bustled around, carrying boxes of supplies and ammunition. Across the docks there was a large gate saying: 'Welcome To Icrises'. People walked to and from the town and the docks, families and sailors.

I was escorted by the men at arms on the ship towards the exit where a horse drawn carriage pulled up, ready to take me to the barracks. I got in and the carriage started to move towards the centre of town. The people of Kakuri had not changed one bit. The market place was as busy as usual, people shouting out to the crowds to come and buy their supplies. Some people were standing on little podiums in the middle of crowds, shouting out their beliefs.

After that there was a church, with people filing in. The religion in Icrises was a complicated affair, with more than ten main faiths. I tried to stay as far away as possible, as I did not want it to get in the way of my job. The punishments were strict and sometimes you were even expelled for believing in a religion. I did not want to get involved.

Five minutes later, we arrived at a long wooden fence that marked the beginning of the military base. The fence turned in to make a large road leading to the gate where they would check your papers and let you in.

Soon we had arrived at the poll gate and the driver had asked me to dismount. I walked up to the wooden barricade and turned, knocking at the glass. A man with a large brown beard walked up with a tired expression on his face. "Papers?" he asked, holding out his hand through the hole in the glass. I looked around in my pockets and soon my hands felt something rectangular and I brought it out for the guards to see. He nodded and walked out of the door in the side to open the gate with his keys. It slowly opened and I walked in towards my barracks.

People around me were training and I saw sweat running down their faces and someone with a large scar across his face. He had obviously been in more battles than I could imagine being in, even though I had tried three times to retake North Trelinster. I saw a sign saying to barracks D to F. My barracks called E, so I followed the path down to my home.

People looked at me with a funny expression on their faces, as I was a rare visitor here. Soon I found my barracks. It was a simple affair, with corrugated iron as a roof and wooden planks as walls. Inside, there was a small fire at the back and four metal bunk beds with the covers nicely made. I rarely came here, so the men that lived here usually would know me, but would need some reminding of who I am.

The other people that inhabited the barracks wouldn't be back till late as the training and exercises wouldn't end till twelve o'clock. I jumped up to the bed nearest to me and threw my belongings up. My bag landed with a satisfying thump. I then crawled up myself and lay on my back and slowly went to sleep...

I woke in the morning and slowly adjusted myself to the light and reminded myself where I was. The other inhabitants had already left for breakfast or training so, again, I was alone. I jumped down and hastily threw my things on, realising that I was late for breakfast.

In ten minutes, I had arrived at the mess hall. The noise was unbearable but I had to deal with it if I was going to meet Corneal Laurence on a full stomach. I went up to the front with a metal barred tray and asked for the breakfast. A rather old lady squinted at me and the put her ladle in the food I had pointed at. She poured the porridge on my bowl and handed it to me, expressionless. I received the bowl had looked for whichever table that had the least people on it.

I managed to find a table with one person, who was at the end who was reading a book and another eating his porridge rather vigorously. I ignored them and put my spoon in the porridge and took a massive mouthful. The porridge felt good. I had not eaten properly since our boat journey to Kakuri.

I turned my head and caught the man opposite me staring and he quickly turned away. I smiled to myself, thinking that all the people here weren't as hard as they made out. I finished my porridge and started for the door. A shout came up from one of the tables I had walked past. Someone yelled: "Look who it is, boys. The person who ruined our future!"

Cheers came up from other tables, but I realised that some of them were quite half-hearted. This man obviously commanded a lot of men and I decided it was best not to start a fight inside a military base, so I ignored him. The man jumped out from his table and held my shoulder while shouting at me saying: "Don't run away from me, scamp. I could snap your bones in one strike!"

As he raised his hands to punch me round the

face, I swung my leg around and hit him dead on the stomach. Enraged by this, he launched another clumsy punch and I dodged it and ran my fist into his face. He fell to the ground, holding his nose.

Cheering rose from the tables around me but I did my best to ignore them as I walked out of the door and went to my appointment, before Corneal Laurence got wind of what just happened.

A car was waiting at the toll gate for me. I walked quickly towards it, hiding the tear in my clothes that the bully had ripped off of me. My ceremonial sword hung loosely from my belt, its diamond encrusted hilt showing. I wore full army dress, without a helmet, as hiding your face was considered a sign of disrespect. I clambered into the car and sat down, making sure my sword wasn't poking into the leather interior.

We started off down a different route from the one we had taken yesterday and I noticed the difference of people as we drove further into the richer areas of Kakuri. The tradition was that corneals were expected to keep their distance from other soldiers. As I was a corneal now, I was probably expected to do that too, but I had grown used to soldiers – especially when I had shared a couple of battles with them as well.

Finally we drew up to HQ. It was an impressive

building, but it looked abandoned as the windows showed no sign of light. Two men at the door noticed me and came to attention and holstered their axes. I nodded, signalling them to relax and they lowered their weapons.

One walked forward and pushed opened the door and light flooded in. I could see a hallway and two doorways leading off. Talk came from the door on the right, so I followed it. As I walked in, I noticed the large table that was being used for pool table. Standing behind it was Corneal Laurence and his two senior officers. I stood to attention but was reminded that I was now equal in rank to Corneal Laurence. The two officers saluted me, obviously remembering what rank I was.

Corneal Laurence shook his head in disappointment. "We certainly got destroyed there, didn't we. After all the men we committed, and all the resources we supplied, we still failed in our quest. What shall we do now, Corneal Sam?" he said. He stressed the word *Corneal*.

"I don't know, sir. As you said, we committed all of our troops to that campaign but, as usual, it failed. They outwitted us, sir." I said, the sorrow laid thick on my voice.

"DON'T SAY THAT! YOU CALL YOURSELF A CORNAEL, BUT YOU BELIEVE THAT THEY

OUTWITTED US! THEY MOST CERTAINLY DID NOT!" He yelled back at me, the anger flooding out.

"I'm very sorry, sir. But this time it didn't pull off." I replied, trying to hold my own anger back.

"Sorry isn't going to bring back the 1,500 men from the dead! I've got a mission for you, and it's a kind of punishment. The details will be at your barracks the moment you get back!" Then he gestured at me to leave, his anger finally spent.

As I turned to leave, he spoke again. "And please stop getting into fights. You'll make every one hate you."

So I left Sinwood Manor and got in the car that was waiting for me on the drive. The driver, seeing that I was upset, opened his mouth to ask something but shut it again suddenly. I was excited to find out what the mission was but, remembering Corneal Laurence's voice, I guessed that this was not going to be fun.

V

The reception at the barracks was not very welcoming. People shied away from me; worrying that – if they made a sort of kind gesture towards me – they would have all the army's bullies against them too.

I made no attempt to apologise to the man that I punched in the face. I walked past a bunch of frightened people before I reached my barracks and, by the time I did, I was hoping to get out of there as soon as possible. I knew the mission was not going to be very good, but anything was better than hanging out here in this god forsaken place, where everyone either hated me or was afraid of me.

I then remembered about the letter that Corneal Laurence had mentioned. I found it at the door, wrapped in a brown envelope, with a label on it saying: 'TO BE OPENED ONLY BY SAM SMITH'.

I peeled open the wrapping and read the inside. *'If you are reading this now, you have been selected for a special mission to help your country and clan to win this war against the Trelinsters. This mission requires courage and we hope you are up to it. The mission is as follows. You are needed to sneak into the capital of Trelinster and find out information about where their troops are positioned along the border. After you find this information, you are to get on an aership disguised as a merchant ship and sneak out of Trelinster. If you return without the information, you will be put to death for failing your nation. Good luck.'*

I was pretty surprised, I can say. This was suicide. They were asking people to wander off into our enemies' country, find a little information and then escape. I couldn't refuse, though, as the punishment for that would be being hanged. It also said that a car would be waiting for me to take me to the dockside tomorrow morning at 5am.

I decided it would be best if I went and got some sleep. Something told me that I wouldn't be getting much of that where I was going.

I woke to the sound of knocking at the door. I looked at the clock next to me and saw that it was 4.30am. A man walked in and yelled "GET UP! YOU NEED AN EARLY BREAKFAST!" then he turned around and left. Realising that this was another thing that I wouldn't be getting a lot of where I was going, I jumped out of bed, got dressed, put on my weapons and went outside.

It was still dark and nobody was up. I thanked the man that shouted at me because otherwise I would be in the mess hall later with everyone that hates me. I hurried along towards the hall and walked in. It was empty apart from the couple of cooks at the end of the room, preparing a breakfast for me. I ran up and collected it.

I licked my lips at the sausages and bacon along with mushrooms steaming on my plate. This time there was no noise other than the cook cooking on the other side of the hall, hissing coming from the pan. I tucked in, shoving spoonfuls of sausages and bacon in my small mouth. They were unbelievably good.

The cook looked over at me and his face turned into a smile when he saw me enjoying his food. The breakfast was finished in a moment and I walked off, leaving my plate at the table for him to clear up.

The letter was right, as a car was waiting for me at the dockside. I clambered in. The driver looked at me with an uncertain face, as if he knew that I was probably never coming back.

The drive back to the docks was much more sullen than before, as I couldn't think of anything else but the suicidal mission that had been bestowed on me, just because I had failed a campaign. The market was empty and no one was going to the church. It looked like a ghost town, in the early hours of the morning.

Soon we arrived at the docks, which, like all the rest of the town, was empty apart from one crew filling up a merchant ship. I guessed that that was the ship that was going to take me to my death. I got out of the car and walked towards it. I showed the letter and they let me on board, warning me to be quiet as we entered enemy territory.

We set sail an hour later and I was stowed below. I was shown a hole at the bottom of the airship, where I would be ordered to jump from when the word was given. I was handed my parachute and left alone to enjoy what would probably be the remaining three hours of my life.

A cannon sounded. I heard wood being ripped apart upstairs and I rushed up to help. People were screaming all around me and I knew our little plot to sneak in to enemy territory had failed.

I peered into the distance and saw two large cruisers coming towards us, guns blazing. The mast fell and smashed the wood underneath it. As the enemy ships drew closer, I realised that these were not Trelinster ships. They were from Senetea. I had seconds to live. I heard a smashing noise and the back of the aership fell into the clouds, taking several people with it. Then I had an idea. I fastened my parachute to my waist, then gripped two grappling hooks. Then I jumped off the edge of the ship.

VI

I felt the parachute open automatically and I swung into action. I lobbed the two grappling hooks I had taken with me towards the Senetean ship's hull. The wood snapped and I pulled on the ropes. I began to fly towards the ship's hull and stopped myself just in time. I then clambered into the small hole the grappling hooks had made and shuffled towards the corner of the hold. There I stayed until I went slowly to sleep.

I woke to the noise of metal against metal. I heard a clatter of feet upstairs and then someone coming into the hold. I had to manoeuvre myself so the hole stayed hidden, though small amounts of light were still seeping through. I was hiding behind a large crate. The man that had come down walked through all the crates, shining his fiery torch around. I stayed silent, knowing that the smallest amount of noise would mean the end of my life.

After about two minutes, he went back up the

stairs and shut the door behind him, locking it. I peered through the hole and saw that we were approaching a large town. It wasn't Kakuri, but it wasn't a Trelinster port either. It was a Senetean port. I knew that escaping through the door that the man just exited from was impossible. The door was locked and, even if I could break it down, there would be at least half of the crew poised to stop me. I had only one way to get out. The hole that I came in.

I put my head through it and looked down. There was a long drop down to the sandy bottom. The other side was within range of my grappling hook. I knew that I only had one chance at this. I threw the grappling hook. It sailed towards the metal railing and I gasped as I saw the line become taught. I knew that someone must have noticed the line flying from the aership, so I had no time to lose. Making sure I had all my weapons, I jumped and pulled myself onto the line, slowly edging my way towards the dock side. People started to point but luckily no one had told the patrol. Yet.

It was now less than a quarter of the way left to the side but, as I glanced towards the dock, I saw men in black and red uniform run towards my objective. The local patrol. I looked in horror as they raised their guns in a neat line and took aim. I quickened my pace along the rope. I looked to the side just in time to see the captain say load and I knew it was too late.

Except that, suddenly, I had an idea. I pulled my knife from its scabbard and raised it above the rope. "FIRE!" Said the captain. And just as I heard the gunshots, I cut the rope. I fell towards the bottom, hoping the rope would hold on the other edge. I neatly swung down to the bottom of the docks and ran for the nearest ladder.

I saw the guns reloading and prayed to Haylir that they would miss. I had now reached the ladder and was swiftly climbing it. Half of the group had rushed to the top and were drawing their swords to stop me climbing onto the top. I drew my own sword.

The guns fired and I flattened myself against the ladder. The bullets whistled past me and I continued my climb. The last bit of the ladder was in sight and I jumped into the line of five people and sliced my sword forward. I cut through the first person and charged at the next, who put up his sword in defence. I grabbed his hand and twisted it, making him drop his sword. I kicked at his stomach and he fell to the ground.

Another person ran at me and I shot him through the head. I charged at the two remaining men and fired my gun at one leg. He fell to the ground screaming. The other man ran at me, his sword outstretched. I hit it away and thrust my sword at him and it went straight through him.

I pulled my sword out of him and he fell to the ground, already dead.

I looked over towards the other group. One man had run towards the stables. I assumed that he was going to send a message to the main patrol HQ. There was nothing I could do to stop him. I ran towards the wall and climbed over it. The patrol did nothing to stop me. I set off into Oesga, the capital city of Senetea.

VII

The city was about ten times cleaner than Kakuri. It was also much less busy. That was not good, since I didn't really want to be killed. The buildings were painted a brownish colour, as if to disguise the dirt that had been plastered on during years and years of people using the houses as homes.

I found an abandoned house and had set it up as a temporary base. I needed a good source of food and warmth so I set off for the nearest marketplace.

I found one not five minutes away from my new headquarters and immediately set to work stealing from drunken shopkeepers, In less than ten minutes, I had two loaves of bread, two chunks of lamb and one apple. I kept my hood up, knowing that the all the army and patrol men stationed in Oesga were out for the famous Sam Smith, corneal of the mighty Third Division. I made it back to the abandoned pub that I was to call my home for the next few months.

The pub had a large room with an old counter and

empty barrels. Behind the counter were stairs leading down to a cellar where more empty barrels had sat for years. On the other side of the main room was another set of stairs leading up to three rooms, along a small corridor. The owners of the White Crow had obviously left in a hurry since the mattresses still had bedding on them.

I made the largest room mine and cleared the bed of dust. I then went downstairs and went into the kitchen that was a small cluttered room, where I had set down my shopping. I set to work cleaning old bowls then making a soup with the lamp. I then sat down at a dusty table and ate it in a moment, dipping my bread in the delicious broth. I was so exhausted that I fell into a deep sleep in a bed I was sure someone had died in.

I woke late next day, going downstairs to check everything was safe. I peered outside via a window and saw the street empty. The sun was high in the sky and I guessed it was about noon. I knew the first thing I had to do was to set out a way of getting back home. I didn't want to think about what Corneal Laurence would do to me after I failed another mission.

I set out into town, with a cloak pulled over my eyes. Sure enough, there were signs everywhere that had my face on it. I realised I would have to find a dealer that was really crooked to let me through. I was going to have to try.

I began walking through the streets towards the centre of town. I realised that there were probably more people smugglers there than in my new neighbourhood. As I got more and more into town, I noticed that the number of patrols that were stationed here was significantly different from my area. I wondered if I should give up on this plan after all but I there was no other place in this town that I knew would have the kind of traffickers I needed. I also noticed a large, white, domed building.

Before too long, I reached the town centre and set about finding the person I needed. In no time, I found one. I approached him slowly. He looked at me and I nodded, showing that I was interested. He gestured for me to follow him into an alleyway. My hand went to my sword, knowing not to trust these sorts of people. Then he spoke.

"Hello. I am guessing you are wanting to get out of this country. I have good deals. Easy and safe. Which country are you willing to escape to?" he said in a raspy sort of voice. I noticed the word escape and thought that maybe the government was being too pushy.

I replied: "Icrises".

He looked back in surprise. "Are you the one

everyone talking about?" he said.

I was shocked that, in only the space of a day, everybody knew that a 'dangerous villain' was loose on the streets of Oesga. Maybe I couldn't trust this man not to snitch but I realised that that would be a risk I would have to take. I stayed silent. The man nodded and then lowered his hood. A golden helm shined through.

"You, Sam Smith of Icrises, are under arrest." He said. There was a smug look on his face.

VIII

Five armed men jumped out behind cover and surrounded me. "Drop your sword," said the captain of the squad. I did as I was told. I knew that even if I did manage to kill one, there would be five left to take his place. They would shoot me before I could even move.

They marched through the town. I noticed that we were walking towards the large white building. Maybe that was where they kept their prisoners. We arrived at the big building and the captain exchanged a few words with the gatekeeper. He nodded and opened some large steel gates.

He marched me up some stairs and into a large doomed room. At the back of the room there was a small staircase down. At the bottom of the staircase, there was a corridor with cells on either side. The captain opened the cell, threw me inside and walked away.

I realised that these cells must be pretty deep

down, so there would be a large number of guards to make sure no one was tunnelling out. I examined my room. There was a wooden bed to one side and a toilet to the other. There was no light, save for a line of torches in the corridor. I started looking for escape routes. I knew it was a matter of time before the guards became suspicious and came to investigate.

I found nothing. The doors were very sturdy and the walls were made of hard rock. Just as I had predicted, a guard walked in and asked me what I was doing. I said nothing. The guard said: "There's no way out of this prison, you know. Even if you did make it out, you would still have to get through several lines of General's Bodyguard."

I said I doubted that I would find that extremely difficult. The guard looked at me with a funny expression and then took that last sentence as a sign to end the conversation. The guard seemed nice enough, but I couldn't waste any time worrying about making friends in a prison where I might very well spend the last of my days.

I stayed up until I couldn't keep my eyes open. I didn't bother collapsing onto the hard wooden board that I was supposed call my bed. Instead I collapsed onto the stone floor and went into a deep, deep sleep.

I woke up to the sound of screeching. I reached for my sword and then realised where I was. I opened my eyes. And to my surprise, the cell door was lying wide open and, to my surprise, the guard that had tried to have a conversation with me yesterday was standing in in the doorway. I was shocked. Then he spoke. "I was taken into slavery, Sir. I was captured in a scouting mission. But my loyalty still lies with Icrises."

I was dumbfounded. Then it made sense. This man was taken into slavery from the Icrises army, so his loyalties were still with the country of his birth. The job he was doing for Senetea was fake. They were forcing him to do it.

He gestured for me to come. "One of the more loyal guards will have heard that. I must stay here. I will try and hold them back for as long as possible. Here, have this."

He tossed me a large knife. I caught it and ran towards the exit. I wasn't going to get another chance.

At the top of the stairs, I found my first challenge. There was a line of men pointing outwards, away from me. I knew that if I charged forward immediately I was as good as dead. There was a corridor leading the opposite way. That was the only way out. I just hoped that it was an exit.

The corridor led past several doors. I stayed as silent has I could. Then I heard raised voices coming through a large double door. I tiptoed towards the door and put my ear to it.

I was shocked by what I heard.

IX

"The barbarian armies are nothing against our mighty ten thousand," I heard someone say. "Their war chiefs will never join forces."

"Don't be cocky," said another voice. "The barbarian tribes are nothing before us, but do NOT underestimate them."

Then another voice. "Don' worry. By next month, we will own the whole world and barbarians will be crushed under our feet."

What were they talking about? Did they really have ten thousand men at the ready? Were they really going to crush the barbarian tribes? Corneal Laurence might be cross with me for failing another mission. But what if I brought him back something better – information that could save the people of Icrises and the others from becoming slaves?

I had heard enough. I clearly had a week to relay this information back to Icrises. I started to tiptoe through the corridor. Finally, I saw daylight shining through an old fire exit. The problem was that two armed guards stood in the way of my freedom. I crept up to their behind. I drew my knife. I cut through the person's back. He cried out in pain. The other man, saw what I had done to his comrade, and yelled for help. In a second, he was on the floor too, lying on his own blood.

I stepped over the two bodies and looked behind me. Ten men were rushing towards me. I ran.

I leapt down a flight of stairs and into a street. The men that were following me were catching up and I did not want to caught again, especially when I had a very important message for Corneal Laurence.

Then a piece of paper fluttered off the end of the knife. I caught it in my hands and read it without slowing down. *I have left you a one-man aership. Use it to get out of this country now.*

I used the signs to get to the docks. The patrol following me had given up and was probably waiting for reinforcements. Soon I was in the docks that I had arrived in. I saw a little one-man aership and ran for it. The Port Master tried to stop me, but I pushed him aside.

Soon, a group of 30 men arrived at the docks and fired their guns. Bullets whizzed past me. I clambered in the driver's seat and cut the ropes. The ship whizzed away, into the sky. My new friend had kindly inflated the balloon for me.

I used the compass to move myself north. The little ship moved surprisingly fast.

I was also surprised to see no enemy ships following. I just needed to reach the border of Icrises and I would be safe. Even the Senetea ships would hardly dare enter our territory without an entire army. They knew that our forces are unrelenting and powerful. But nothing would stop their army now.

Soon, I saw the bustling town of Kakuri. I slowly lowered the small ship down towards the dock. I docked automatically, leapt out and started to run for a taxi. I jumped in one and asked for Sinborn Manor.

They drove annoyingly slowly but there was nothing I could do. I just had to pray that everybody believed my story. It was quite far-fetched. Any story involving ten thousand men was a bit unlikely. And after my failure in my last mission I doubted that Corneal Laurence would be able to believe me.

The taxi pulled up outside Sinborn Manor and opened the door for me. I nodded and gave the taxi driver ten crowns. Then I slowly walked up the flight of steps leading to Icrises army headquarters. I pushed open the door and saw Corneal Laurence standing there admiring a painting on the wall. He turned to see who it was that was ruining his thinking time, getting ready to shout.

But when he saw it was me, the words didn't come out. "S-s-smith?" he said.

X

"What are you doing here, Smith? You're supposed to be in North Trelinster!" he exclaimed.

"Sorry Sir. Senetea Ships attacked the ship that I was being transported on. I was taken prisoner." I left out the bit where I ran away.

He looked at my clothes and nodded. "I believe you. But why do you come back to me?"

"I have urgent news, Sir. Senetea is massing an army ten thousand strong. They plan to crush the barbarian tribes." A servant came in and offered me a drink. I took it and gulped it down.

"That's stupid. Senetea would never do something like that. Have you no proof?"

I realised that this was going to be the biggest problem. "No, Sir. I overheard the officers discussing it as I escaped."

"And how did you escape?"

"A slave there helped me. He was once an Icrises

solider, until he was captured."

"How did you get captured, by the way?"

I now had to tell him everything. So I began.

"A group of two ships ambushed us and laid waste the two ships that we owned. I sneaked onto the enemy ship and hid in the hold until I arrived somewhere. I then peered out of the window and saw that I had arrived in Oesga. I fled the ship. I made a base in an abandoned inn called the White Crow."

One of the servants looked up suddenly but then lowered his head down. I continued: "I went out to find people smugglers but the local patrol caught me. They threw me in a cell. One of the guards helped me out. It was on my way out that I overheard the Senetea officers speaking about the upcoming invasion. I rushed to a one-man aership and here I am."

"Lies!" yelled Corneal Laurence.

Then the servant looked up again. "No, Sir. I used to live in Senetea. I know this to be true. The pub he made his base was mine."

XI

Preparations for war had begun. The main army was called back from its campaign in North Trelinster and the aerships were moved back to Kakuri. But still our army didn't even match the size of the enemy's. We would need more.

Our only hope was to convince the other clans to join us. But since all of them hated us, I doubted that they would willingly join in beside us. We needed another way to convince them. I quickly sent a telegraph to all the other barbarian clans. Hopefully they would come to Icrises and, if they did, I then would go to them.

I was sitting in the barracks waiting for a reply, as I had been for the last week. Then finally, a letter. There was a metallic noise as the letterbox was pushed open and then a thud as a letter hit the floor. I rushed to see what it was. A brown letter with no stamps on it lay on the floor. I picked it up and levered the flap up. I pulled on a piece of paper and it came out neatly. I examined it then read the first line.

From the State of Balbar.
   We have read your letter and think that such peace in impossible. The state of Balbar wishes to protect its own. However, the ten thousand men threat coming from Senetea is a big one. We have sent spies to see and they have returned with dire news. The army is indeed large and it seems that they are preparing for war. We will not allow you to come to us but we will offer a compromise. We will meet a Temple's Point in South Trelinster to discuss matters.

I was glad that Balbar had agreed to meet us. It meant that they knew what danger they all were in. I moved to clear up the brown envelope that it had come in, when another piece of paper fell out. This time it was from Trelinster.

From the State of Trelinster,
   We all know a threat so big that it could crush a nation has been unleashed on the world. We all know that we cannot fight it alone. We are willing to meet with you and Balbar to discuss the threat and somehow come to an agreement. Balbar has

already contacted us about where to meet. We will meet you there in five days. Be there.

The surprise that both letters came at the same time faded away to the realisation that a treaty was possible. I had to rush this information over to HQ as soon a possible. We would have to sent the war chief along with all the corneals. Also a group of fifty men would also have to come.

But it was possible. Everything was.

XII

Once Corneal Laurence had seen the letters, he sent for the war chief, Chief Caine Waeholl. We gathered our best men and got two cruisers ready for the journey to South Trelinster. South Trelinster was one of the lands that lay the closest to Senetea, so it was always under threat from Senetea.

It was a snowy and bleak landscape with icy peaks. Temples Point was one of those, a cold mountain. It was one of the only neutral areas of the entire world. Inside was what used to be a thriving frontier fort. It has now been reduced to nothing after the Great Invasion from Balbar. It now lay empty but it could come in useful, as it did in this particular instance.

We set off for South Trelinster the next morning, with an envoy of fifty of our best men. The war chief, Caine Waeholl, was a large man with not a great deal of armour. All he wore was a linen jacket embroidered with gold. A hammer was strapped to his back. It was named Gorestick and he carried it everywhere. A beard grew down his face. He was riding a small white pony with four men with golden armour on surrounding him. They rode horses, also wearing golden armour. They all carried axes and a golden shield with their clan sign on it.

The twelve corneals, including me, rode in front and behind of the war chief. Twenty-five men rode in front of us. Five food caravans rode in front of the twenty-five and then, in front of them, lay another twenty-five men.

The road to South Trelinster went along the mountains knows as the Bohama Range. These peaks went down the side of Icrises and down into the neutral area. The air grew cold and warm coats were distributed. Finally, after three long days of riding, Temples Point came in view. Temples Point was as depressing as ever, the crumpled city spires pointing above the icy peaks.

The fort had a wall surrounding it, as well as a natural, icy wall behind that. I caught a glimpse of the other approaching armies and I naturally reached for my sword. Corneal Laurence, who was situated next to me and eyed me. I lowered my hand and went back to guiding my pony down the steep incline that led to Temple's Point.

As we entered the old city, a sense of foreboding

fell over us. The dark ruined buildings loomed over us, with the sense of death all around. The Chieftain's Bodyguard drew close together to protect him from anything that might seek to do him harm. We followed the main gate up to the town hall where we agreed to meet. We dismounted and closed in around the chief.

The town hall was a large building with stained glass and a large door made out of metal stood in the way. It looked like it was meant for defence, not beauty. Inside, there was a large table with candles all around the room.

The other factions had already arrived and were sitting around the table. They had their bodyguards and corneals situated around them. We sat down in the middle and the corneals gathered around our war chief.

Balbar started. "As we all know Senetea is amassing a giant army to crush the factions. It is our job to stop that. We MUST set aside our differences and work together for the greater good."

The war chief of Trelinster stood up. "We all know such peace to be impossible. The army is too big. We will be crushed if we stand against the armies of Senetea!"

Caine rose. "THIS IS THE KIND OF DEFEATISM THAT WILL LOSE US THIS WAR!" he shouted.

The war chief of Trelinster, Barld Goel, rose again. "That is your problem. I do not see why we should lend out aid!"

I said quickly: "Because if you do not, we will all fall."

"Who is this stripling that dares speak to the mighty Barld Goel?" asked one of the Trelinster bodyguards.

I continued, ignoring him: "Do you not see that we must band together to defeat the armies of Senetea? As Balbar said, we must set our differences aside and work for the greater good. Who's with me?"

The chief of Balbar rose and came to stand near us. His bodyguards followed him. Caine stood and nodded to me. On the other side of the room, Trelinster stood alone. A corneal whispered in Barld's ear. Barld nodded and said: "Trelinster is with you. I hope this is not a fool's errand."

XIII

The other factions called for an army to aid us. We would march north tomorrow. But, for now, it was up to us to find accommodation for the night. Most of the buildings still stood and had walls still standing.

We decided to stay in the building closest to the wall so we were ready when reinforcements came. We organised a guard to keep watch and the bodyguards closed in around the war chief. I was on first watch and knelt outside the black-stone building that we had made our base. We had lit a couple of fires and people were huddling around them and roasting food. It had been a long day but, for me, it was not over yet.

The first I heard was a roar and a crash. Screaming echoed around me. I looked around me. Fire was spreading and a rock was imbedded in a building next to us. I rushed out of bed and reached for my sword and armour. I put it on quickly and ran towards Corneal Laurence, who was kneeling over a fallen solider. "What's happening? Has something happened between the factions?" I asked, shouting over the chaos.

"War," he said as he turned to face me. "The Seneteans have arrived and are attacking. We have been caught unawares. We number only two hundred. Their forces triple ours. Rush to the walls. Alert the war chief that we are leaving along with the other factions." He turned back to his dying comrade.

I left Corneal Laurence, realising he was no use in a situation like this. I ran towards the gate. The Trelinster soldiers had formed a barricade with their spears, and Balbar troops were hiding behind them, sniping off any Senetea men that left the safety of their group.

I ran past a few fights and found the war chief, fighting three men along with his personal bodyguards. His hammer ripped into one of them and flung him aside like a rag doll. The next person ran at him, but he knocked him aside with a shield. The third person, seeing what had happened, ran. He did not get far. A bullet pierced his hide and he fell to the ground, already dead.

I rushed to the war chief. "Sir, we need to withdraw. They have surrounded us."

He nodded. "Sound the retreat!" he yelled at the nearest bodyguard.

We ran towards the town hall. Trelinster had informed us of a secret passage leading out of the city and under the mountains. They knew the way. I saw Corneal Laurence join the hundreds of fleeing men running to get out of the town. I looked behind us and saw hundreds of Senetean soldiers running towards us, cutting people down as they came. The town hall was burning to add to the chaos.

We piled into the burning building and barricaded the door, giving us some time to get ready and prepare for the long walk ahead of us. A Trelinster bodyguard walked over to a bookshelf and shoved it over. We all gasped. A small passageway led out of the building and into the mountain. Torches lit the way.

The remainder of us ran forward and into the tunnel. The last person to get in took a torch and threw it at the ground. A wall of fire appeared and we started to jog into the darkness.

XIV

Wooden supports held up the passage. They looked like they were going to collapse at any moment; the crumbling was evident. The tunnel had not seen people in hundreds of years. The group of 150 men huddled together in a long line. We walked solidly for hours until someone up ahead called "Halt!"

We all flung ourselves to the ground and broke out the rations. I broke a piece of bread apart and dipped it in the cold soup.

After an hour of resting, it was back on the road. The bodyguards told us it was another two hours until we would see light. The plan was to move back to the capital of Trelinster and regroup there. When we had prepared ourselves, we would march to Kakuri and prepare for battle. Each faction was giving about 3,000 men to help. They still outnumbered us though. We would have to use all our courage and strategy to get us past this one.

The bodyguard was right. In the next two hours,

we saw light. We started to run towards the exit, but the people in front stopped them. The person at the very front peered around the exit. Two men stood there looking out. The armour showed that they were Senetean solders. He gestured for two people to come with him. He drew his knife silently, and cut his throat.

It was over in a second. He looked around for any more and ran out of the cave. People followed him. I exited the cave and looked up. Temples Point loomed above us, burning. I bowed my head in respect and headed over to Corneal Laurence. He nodded at me and turned back to the war chief, discussing matters of war. I sheathed my sword and got ready for the long ride down to Trelinster's capital, Inida.

The remaining 150 men trudged along the snowy pass down the mountains. The food had been rationed out and a carrier pigeon had been send to Inida calling for aid. At the front of the short column were the three war chiefs, discussing plans to hold the army of Senetea at bay.

Soon the city of Inida was in sight. Most of the column gasped. The city was more industrial than any city I had ever seen, the chimneys launching out into the atmosphere. Fires rose into the sky, some industrial and some real fires. Some houses had been burned to a cinder. There was nothing left of those houses. Some still burned, people desperately trying to put them out but to no avail. The walls of the city stood firm and in the distance stood the keep, the wooden castle dominating the city. On the keep, stood the Trelinster flag, a dove carrying a sword in its beak. "It symbolises that peace cannot be achieved without war," said a Trelinster solider next to me. I nodded.

We rode down the mountains and towards the gate. The few soldiers that were guarding it looked tiered and yanked at the rope that controlled the gate. It swung open and a lone rider rode out of the city. He dismounted and bowed to the respective war chiefs.

"Welcome to Inida City. We hope you will enjoy your stay. Now, as you can see, we are having trouble with air raids. In the night, Senetean ships dart in, drop bombs and dart back out. In the inky black darkness of the night we can't chase them and destroy them fast enough, so we were going to ask to borrow a few Icrises ships to defend our city and thus keeping the factories online. We all know how fast they are."

The war chief nodded. "We will give you five frigates. I will send for them now."

"Now gentlemen, if you would follow me. We have much to discuss."

The lone rider rode back into the gate and gestured for us to follow. We spurred our horses into a gallop and rode after him. Our war chief rode slowly behind us, shadowed by his bodyguard. As we rode, we passed burning houses and children living rough on the streets. Some people booed as we passed and some cheered. A man who was cradling a dead baby in his arms, reached down and put her to rest. Tears started to well in his eyes and he looked up.

His gaze settled on the war chief. He ran, screaming at the top of his lungs, towards him. Just has was about to reach the war chief, the bodyguard leapt into action. The one closest to the attacker drew a knife and knelt, cutting at the assailant's legs. He fell to the ground, screaming. The Trelinster solders quickly ran up and carried away the body.

Caine Waeholl spared the screaming man a nod and continued to ride on. The war chief of Trelinster spat on the floor, his expression full of disgust. We rode past the burned-out castle. The Corneal next to me nudged me.

We rode into the gates and past the lines of trenches, to a bunker. We dismounted. As I walked down the steps, I realised how strong this thing could be against an attack. The building was made entirely out of metal, even the door. In the middle of the room, there was a table with a map of the world on it. Little mini-figures stood on the table, representing legions. Around the table there were chairs. The war chief gestured for us to sit down. "According to our information, the Senetean army will be at Kakuri in two weeks," he said. "They are ten thousand strong and, as we are now, we will fall."

"Why not leave Kakuri? We will feint a retreat and then ambush them when they are disorganised?" said a Trelinster corneal.

"No. They will be expecting that," replied the war chief of Balbar. People nodded.

"How many men do we have?" asked an Icrises corneal.

"We have 7,000, not counting the scout parties that are spying on the enemy," said the Trelinster war chief.

"I have an idea, if you would listen," said Caine Waeholl. "We march to Kakuri in a week, giving us a week to prepare. While we are marching, we recruit people from the villages we pass. When we arrive in Kakuri, we call back the scouts. Also by then, the Balbar army will have reached Kakuri." The majority of the corneals nodded but I saw a few who shook their heads.

The Trilenster war chief rose. "All in favour of this idea, raise your hands," he said. Most people raised their hands in response. "Then it is decided. We march for Kakuri in seven days. Prepare."

XV

The bustling city of Inida was even more busy in the next seven days. I had been ordered to lead the five frigates which had arrived in Inida the previous day into battle against the raiding ships. They had not been lying about the wreckage they had caused either, I thought as I climbed up the gangplank to the RIAS *Spearhunter*.

The ship was a small one, with ten cannons on either side, and two machine guns at the front. There were two decks and a captain's quarters. Above that, there was a viewing platform where the steering wheel was located. I stepped onto the ship and climbed up the ladder to the viewing platform, where the captain awaited me.

"Good weather for flying, Sir," he said to me without turning round.

"Yeah." I nodded.

I then turned to the dockside and yelled to the rest of my squadron. "ALL ABOARD! LET GO THE

ROPES!" Promptly, the ropes were untied and the balloon inflated and we rocketed up in the air. The whirring of the engine started and we set off towards the city border, where we would wait for the bombing raid. I signalled for the other four ships to follow. Soon the RIAS *Axethrower*, *Swordholder*, *Gunshooter* and *Wolfowner* set off to their destinations.

Two hours later, it all started. At first, it was a boom, and the sound of screaming, and then the sound of engines escaping into the night. We signalled with torches for the other ships to follow us, making sure that no noise was emitted. We followed them well for ten minutes, making no noise. That was when a cannon blast rocketed the ship.

Our ships opened fire immediately. The ship rocked from side to side, firing all of its ten cannons. The other four ships behind us drew up in a line and all fired their cannons. People rushed past me, carrying stretchers or buckets of water. I rushed up to the viewing platform. Our ship had been hit in two places, shattering the rudder.

"FULL AHEAD! STAND BY TO REPEL BORDERS!" I yelled down to the sailors amidst the noise and smoke. They nodded and called out the order to the engine room below us.

We were sailing towards the enemy ships,

dodging cannon fire. Men rushed to the railings, drawing their weapons and shouting their battle cries. The men on the other ship lined up with their muskets. One, two, three...

Bullets fired and soldiers leaped onto the enemy ship. I yelled and jumped, landing squarely in front of a attacking solider. I sliced at him and he fell to the ground. I drew my pistol and fired at a lone man hiding behind a barrel, where he must have been sniping at people. He fell to the ground as I ran into the fray, reloading my pistol.

I parried an attack from the right and kicked at the assailant, sending him flying across the deck. I then fired my gun, taking down a charging solider. I roared at the remaining people and charged a fleeing man. I cut him down and fired my pistol again, felling the captain, who was desperately trying to turn the ship around. I yelled to fall back. As I jumped back onto the safety of the *Spearhunter*, the ship behind me fell as ten cannonballs smashed into its hull.

The other fights were going as well as could be expected, but one of our ships had been blown up by a well-placed shot to the magazine. I ordered the squadron to get behind the remaining enemy ships and fire our musket and cannons. We lined up behind the railings and fired our muskets.

Their remaining ships were taken by surprise. The first ship fell down to the snowy hill below the last one and swiftly surrendered. We cheered and set off towards Inida, blowing up the remaining ship after rescuing the surrendered soldiers on it.

The dockyard was empty, save a couple of families who had arrived to see how their loved ones survived. There was cheering and crying. I left the ship sadly; even though it had been a victory, we had lost twenty good men, and of course there had been the ship that we had lost.

The other nights had been uneventful. After the crushing defeat, the Senetean ships had retreated their base. I had moved ten ships to the city border to ward off any more raids. I doubt that they would try another assault without a substantial number of ships, but being cautious never hurt anybody.

Finally, the order came through. The 6,000 men that we had prepared were waiting outside the gates, preparing for the two-day march to Kakuri. Supply ships and aerships waited above, their crew saluting as the war chiefs rode below them.

The army folded in on itself as they rode through. Horns sounded and the gates creaked open. And so it began.

XVI

The march to Kakuri was a long one. Every two hours we rested, ate and then we set off again. We came prepared with more than enough food. The men were rationed, but were given three meals a day. The mood was jolly, each solider talking to the man next to himself.

We reached Kakuri in three days. The red-painted gates were left open and the patrolling ships saluted us as we rode below them. The gates slammed shut and the soldiers were showed to their barracks. At the harbour, Balbarian ships docked and soldiers flooded out of the ships and were given a tour of the town, to show them the lay of our defences.

Five aerships departed, carrying civilians to safety. We started to dig trenches and set up barricades at the gate and set up some other defences. We sent a hundred men up to the watch post and set up some cannons. As more men rushed into the city, the final army from Balbar arrived. We were ready.

We heard them first. Like a bunch of elephants. They had left a scar in the land they passed, leaving the villages empty. The citizens were given fair warning and carts came to pick up the people that wanted to leave, but same preferred to stay in the towns that they had spent most of their life in. The soldiers rushed to the walls and the cannoners rushed to their stations.

The aerships took flight and we readied ourselves for battle. One. Two. Three. The cannons launched their explosives and the enemy army rushed forward.

Ladder were swung up to the walls and oxen started to lead a ram through the troops. We cut down the ladders almost as fast as they could throw them up. My squad and I were positioned on the west wall. As the siege towers grew closer, I heard the ram hit the gate with a thud. Men rushed up to the gate and flung up wooden boards, to make it sturdier. I heard guns being loaded and I held up my hand, to signal them to wait.

Below us, solider lowered their pikes at the gate, ready to stop the hordes of people that would come surging in if the ram succeeded. The cannons focused their fire on the siege towers and many fell but still more came. I lowered my hand and loaded my own gun. I nodded and the twenty-five people next to me raised their muskets. I yelled and the twenty-five muskets fired.

The door slammed down and people charged out. I fired again and then charged into battle. The first slash came at me and I parried and kicked at the assailant, sending him sprawling to the floor. I came down on him and neatly thrust my sword into his gut. I then grabbed a torch and threw inside the siege tower, making it burst into flames and topple to the ground, crushing the people below.

The remaining people swiftly surrendered and we prepared for the second attack. The dead bodies were swiftly moved to a safer place to be burned. The stench of rotting flesh was already floating in the air.

As tower after tower came down on the walls, we realised that they would keep on coming. We needed a different plan. I ordered spikes to be placed on the area that the towers landed on. As the tower door slammed open, people were already screaming as they fell onto the metal poles that had been planted. The remaining men inside the tower now struggled to get back into the safety of the siege tower. Then a couple of well placed cannon balls and the entire thing fell to the ground, killing everybody inside.

Realising that the assault on the walls was failing, the Senetean troops fell back and the assault on Kakuri entered its second phase.

The only part of the attack that had gone well for them was the gate. The gate was splintered in several places and we had had to reinforce it with wooden boards. Another corneal took my watch and I retired to my chambers. I fell straight to sleep, not letting the yells and cries of battle disturb me in my sleep.

By God, I would need it.

XVII

I was awakened by a pulling at my shoulder.

"Sir! Sir!" called a squeaky voice, which could only be the barrack's servant. "Yes... What is it?" I mumbled, slowly opening my eyes.

"Sir! They have broken the gate. Hundreds of men are flooding though. We have been forced to retreat to the first line of defences."

I got hurriedly dressed and woke the other corneals that had been taking their sleep alongside me. I told them the news and we hurried onto the courtyard overlooking the city.

The servant had been right.   Hundreds of Senetean soldiers stood on the ramparts. And I looked in dismay as I saw the trenches that we had built and the troops desperately holding on. I nodded at the corneals around me and together we ran into the action.

As I drew my sword, Corneal Laurence called out my name from down in the trenches. "Smith!

Smith!" I looked down and jumped into the trenches, sending mud everywhere. Men lined the walls of it, each looking for an opportunity for a shot. Charges where continually coming but, every time, we mowed them down with a well placed cannon blast.

"Sir?" I nodded at Corneal Laurence.

"As you can see, we're in a sticky predicament. The charges never reach the trenches but, if one does, the entire line will fall. The Seneteans take no prisoners so, if they take a trench, we lose five hundred men and we fall back to Defences Line No.2." He caught his breath.

I said: "If we continue like this, we will run out of ammunition and be overrun. Why don't we just gather our forces and charge at the gate? The enemy doesn't have any defences and they will not have any cannons yet."

"By God, that's it! You're a genius, Smith! I will ready the forces for an attack!"

"Thank you, Sir. Just doing my duty." A horn sounded and the hundred men that we had gathered inside the trench and prepared to charge the enemy lines.

One. Two. Three. The sound of a gunshot and we charged over the trenches, yelling our defiance. The enemy was taken completely by surprise and didn't have time to fire their muskets before we were on them. I shot my pistol and cut down a soldier that was desperately trying to reload his gun. He fell to the ground and I picked up the gun and, with a flick of a switch, fired at the next person in sight. He fell, screaming in pain.

I dropped the musket to the floor and sliced at the charging person. He parried my slash and ducked, and ran at my legs, throwing me to the ground. He drew his sword and thrust it downwards. I rolled out of the way just in time and kicked myself up. I sliced again but this time he was unprepared. He knelt down and the slice went neatly over his head. I kicked at his head and he went toppling over just in time for me to put a well placed bullet though his chest.

I looked around and the remaining men were fleeing towards the gate. More men came pouring out of the trenches and quickly set up base. Cannons were pulled up to the gates and they were quickly shut. Cheering went up and for once I felt happy.

XVIII

Outside the city, the Senetean army was still there, planning their next move, or so I understood later.

"I thought you said the clans were never going to join up! What are we going to do now?" asked General Blokmid.

"Do not fret. Even if the clans have made a treaty, we still outnumber them. No one can stop the might of the Senetean Army. Send word to Captain White. Tell him to move in. Go!" said Senator Hans.

The young general saluted and left the tent. "There can only be one victor in this war."

A mile away, a disappointed Sam Smith was marching his division towards the docks. I had been ordered to guard this area with three other Balbarian divisions. I wanted to be at the first trench, holding the line against the invaders but instead I was guarding this boring place. I knew too well what would happen if the port were to fall but I did not want to be the one defending it.

It was well into the night when I first heard the splash of water against wood and whispers. I woke with a start and ran to the nearest Balbarian corneal.

"Do you hear that?"

He nodded and swiftly woke the other corneal. The noise was getting closer and soon would be upon us. I drew my sword and woke my ten men. They drew their swords and prepared for what was coming down the river. Then we heard it. The sound of someone running up the beach.

"Ready..." I whispered. And then they were upon us.

The noise of steel against steel echoed around. I ran to the bell and rang it three times. As I prepared to ring it the fourth time, a bullet whistled past my shoulder and axe came down on me. I parried it just in time and slid down the beach, under my attacker.

I swung my sword up between his legs and cut him in two. We were outnumbered and were being pushed up the beach. I swung my sword and cut down the nearest person but more came.

Then, suddenly, I had an idea. Slipping away from the fighting, I crept down the beach and grabbed one of the braziers. I pulled it neatly of the wall and flung it at the nearest ship. It caught aflame almost immediately and the crew rushed up on deck to try and put it out, but to no avail.

I ran back to the fighting and cut down two from behind, taking them by surprise. Cheering went up through the remaining men as the fiery boat tipped over and the mast fell onto the next ship spreading the fire. Smoke rose above the harbour buildings and flew into the night sky.

The attackers, unnerved that their only means of escape was burning, pushed on and no matter how many we cut down, they kept on pushing us up the beach, until we finally hit the road. The road lay beneath a cliff, below the city. The gravel track weaved its way up the cliff where a gate stood.

"SPREAD OUT. SINGLE FILE, BLOCK THE ROAD!" I yelled at the thirty men that had survived the surprise attack. The remaining men followed their orders and spread out, doing as I said. The attackers regrouped down the hill to reorder themselves. They slowly marched up the hill and gathered speed, charging at the wall.

"DOWN SWORDS!" I ordered and the men lowered their swords, so the wall of swords was ready.

Just as the men were upon us, I heard a blood-curdling scream and a line of arrows thudded into the first line of attacking soldiers.

"CHARGE!" and a hundred axe-wielding huscarls jumped over us and ploughed into the enemy. The enemy started to flee down the hill but a wave of arrows made sure they didn't get far.

"SMITH!" a joyous voice called out. A delighted Corneal Laurence lumbered towards me, his arms outstretched. He engulfed me in a bear hug and I did the same. We stayed in this position for a moment the broke apart as we made ready to leave for the city centre. My job had been completed. I was to see the war chief and get my next orders. Hopefully they would give me something more challenging.

It was silent. Everything. Even the birds failed to sing. And this was why Sam Smith was sitting on the guard's tower searching for any movement in the dark abyss that was the Waste Lands.

Me and my men had been ordered to look out for any more surprise attacks. But still it was silent. Breakfast was passed around the ten men that I commanded and we all dug into our bacon and eggs like savages.

Below the city prepared for another day of brutal attacks and assaults. The trenches were cleaned and cannons reloaded. The injured soldiers were shipped out via the remaining aerships. They would probably come back too late from their mission of mercy to be of any help.

Suddenly a shudder in the earth woke us up from our sleep, and the second day has begun.

XIX

The Senetean generals would not try a ground assault. We had strengthened our defences a great deal and they would risk a lot of men if they attempted to storm the gate. Ouraerships waited as a fleet of Senetean aerships slowly approached, the cannons stalking their prey.

I clambered down the tower and ran to my ship, the *Dawnbreaker*. The crew stood at the ready and as I boarded, the balloons inflated and we rocketed off the ground, meeting with the other fifty ships.

I climbed the ladder to the bridge and met my ship's mate. He nodded and yelled out: "CANNONS AT THE READY!"

The sailors below us clambered to their action stations and manned the cannons. The mood was tense as the enemy ships turned to get their cannons in line. One. Two. Three...

Our hull was pelted with cannon balls and the

cracking of wood filled the air. "Fire!" I said to my first mate.

"FIRE!" he shouted down. The cannon balls flew away to their target and most hit. The enemy returned fire and soon we were locked in combat with the opposite ship. We had sustained minor damage to the engine and I looked in excitement as the battle raged on. The ship next to me was not having as much luck as me though. The balloon was on fire and the last thing that was holding them up was looking like it was going to overheat.

"JUMP ABOARD!" I yelled across.

The captain turned and nodded and gave the order to abandon ship. My crew rushed to the side to help the fleeing sailors aboard. As they clambered on, their ship started to lean to one side. The captain was thrown to the floor and the cannons broke loose from their bindings. At that moment, the engine exploded and destroyed the hull.

The ship tipped completely to one side and the balloon fell to the ground, setting the floor on fire in seconds. Men jumped off the side and the ship exploded as the fire reached the magazine.

I put my hand up to defend my face as the burning embers were blown towards us. I prayed that none of these bits of flame would land on our ship, because if they did, we would suffer the fate as the aership that had been next to us. I turned the ship away from the burning wreckage of the late aership.

I jumped down from the bridge and landed squarely in front of a cannon. I lit the fuse and the cannon ball whistled away. It hit the enemy ship dead on the engine. Flames engulfed the balloon and the ship blew in half and fell down to the waste land below.

Cheering went up in ship and we turned to look as our flagship, the *Fearsmasher*, signalled the advance. The engine roared to life and we sprung forward, closing in on the enemy lines.

On the other side, the Senetean soldiers lined the cannons and reloaded. Fifty metres until we would be able to board them. Forty. thirty, twenty, ten...

Then all hell broke loose. The grappling hooks shot away to their destination, most of them meeting their target. We were pulled towards the enemy ships and, in just moments, we were there. We drew our shiny swords and leaped across the gap.

I landed straight in front of a sailor who was loading a cannon. He barely had enough time to put his hands up to defend himself when my sword sliced down on his shoulder. He crumpled to the floor and I sought another target.

As if on cue, the captain walked out of his cabin

and cut down a marine. He fell to the ground and I leapt to avenge him. My sword slash narrowly missed the captain, but the second time I brought my sword down on him and he parried with his cutlass. Our eyes met and suddenly he looked down to see my pistol pointed at his gut. "Goodbye..." I whispered in his ear and, with that, I pulled the trigger, sending him flying down the stairs that he had just arrived from not two minutes before.

Around me, the battle was going well. The remainder of their sailors started to subconsciously back away. Little did they know that I was standing right behind them. My cutlass plunged through one sailor's back and I slashed my sword to one side cutting straight through my attacker, without even looking.

The remainder swiftly surrendered and we led them back to the ship after setting fire to the aership. We swiftly cut the ropes and flew away. We wanted to be as far away as possible when the fire that we had started reached the magazine.

Most battles along the line had gone as well, it appeared, and the enemy general sounded the retreat horn. The surviving ships fled towards the safety of their makeshift port. But we would not so easily be fled from. Just as they thought they were safe, a barrage of cannon shots made sure they did not get far. They exploded in a shower of flame and sparks, leaving nothing of them to be remembered by.

The entire Senetean fleet had been destroyed. This had been a crushing defeat for the Senetean high command. They would fall back to their camp and nurse their wounds while they came up with another strategy. We had lost three ships while the enemy had lost fifty.

A attack from the air was now out of the question. Their attack from the sea had already failed. The only thing remaining was an assault from land. And even that had not gone so well for them the first time they tried it. What could they do next? We were about to find out.

XX

All forces were to move to the gate. This was the order that the High Council had given. We were to fortify it and move all cannons there. If the enemy broke though, we were to barrage them with cannon fire then counter charge out of the gate with our entire cavalry unit. If we won the battle, we would win the war. Those were to words of the war chief. I intended to keep my oath and defend the gate and hold the line until it was time to push back.

The mood in the trenches was tense. You could hear the enemy soldiers gathering outside and the ram approaching. Every hit on the gate was like a needle piercing the atmosphere. Nobody wanted them to break through but, in a strange way, we *did* want them to come though. It would shatter the tension and we could concentrate on one thing. Winning the battle and the war.

Soon the gate was on its last legs and the wooden constructs holding it up where slowly crumbling away. Good. About time these cowards showed themselves. It had been three days since the crushing defeat with the aerships and, since then, they had stayed quiet, just like we had predicted. But now they had come. And about time.

The noise when the gates crashed open was unbearable. It was a high pitched screeching sound it was other-worldly. Then, out of the mist came the worst thing that could have come. A Mistweaver.

The four-limbed monster crawled out of the mist, screaming its dreadful scream and thrashing its arms about. These legendary monsters where only mentioned in myth. Already the Fall Back horn was being sounded.

"FALL BACK! FALL BACK TO THE INNER WALL!" I yelled to the people around me. Most people had already started to flee. The cannons had only got one shot off before the Mistweaver smashed them away with one of its four arms.

"RUN! RUN!" I shouted to the remaining men. They turned and nodded. They ran for the gate and I looked down the trench to see if I had left any behind. Nobody.

I climbed up the back wall of the trench and soon was running as fast as my legs could carry me towards the second gate. As I looked back, I saw the Mistweaver's one eye focus on me. And it screamed.

I stopped running and held my hands to my ears. The screaming stopped and the monster started to lumber towards me. I picked myself up from the ground and continued to run towards the gate.

"COME ON! COME ON!" Corneal Laurence yelled from the safety of the wall. I jumped. And I never hit the ground. The monster held me in the palm of his claw and started to squeeze.

I had seconds before I was crushed into a pulp. So I did the only thing I could do. I shot him in the eye. He automatically dropped me to the floor and I gathered myself up again and threw myself into the door.

The gate shut behind me and I started to walk to the command centre. I had no doubt that we were going to have to plan our tactics again.

"Now as you can see, we are in a bad position. With the introduction of the Mistweaver, we are outnumbered and outgunned. We will have to be extremely careful about how we deal with this," said the war chief of Balbar in a low voice. "If they manage to break through the wall, we will fall."

"Why not try and bring the monster down with cannon balls?" asked an Icrises corneal.

"No. The cannon balls just bounce off. Their armour is made of steel. No blade can pierce it and no shot can wound it. The only weak point is the eye, as your colleague just found out," said the Balbar war chief. "And you need to be really high up to shoot it."

It was time I made my suggestion. "We have the height. If we can climb up to the top of the wall we can kill it, then charge the remaining army with our combined cavalry?" I said.

"It's risky and dangerous but if it works it could win us the war. I'm in," said the Trilenster war chief.

"I agree," muttered the Icrises war chief.

"Fine. But don't blame me if this goes horribly wrong," sighed the Balbar war chief.

XXII

I had been elected, obviously, to go on this mission. The war chiefs wished me their best luck and Caine, the war chief for Icrises, gave me a nod, which in his language was Three Cheers.

Cannons lined the walls to distract the monster's attention away from a small man climbed a wall. Me.

I crawled up the wall and threw my two grappling hooks. They locked into position and I launched myself onto the wall, landing squarely in front of the giant. I drew my long-ranged musket, or as long-ranged as a musket can be. It was pre-loaded and I levelled it up to the creature's eye.

The eye swung to meet me. The monster growled and I knew what was coming. Dropping the musket to the floor, I pulled my hands up to my ears, just in time for the screaming to begin. Then it stopped. I looked in horror has the four arms were raised, and then brought down.

I rolled to the side. I knelt down to pick up the

musket, but realised it was gone. I swore under my breath as it tumbled down into the outer city. As I reached to draw my pistol, the pouch was empty. I swore again as I realised I must of left it in the Council Room. Damn.

I drew my sword, the last weapon in my possession. As the arms fell again. I rolled and picked up a bit of rubble. Holding it in my hands, I threw it at the eye and hit it squarely in the middle. The eyelid closed and he started to fall over to one side.

Trusting in luck, I jumped and landed on his shoulder. I crawled up the head and brought the sword down, neatly slicing in and out. The monster groaned and fell on the wall.

The wall was smashed in half and the Mistweaver ground to a halt in front of the remaining army. I jumped down and looked at the bit of wall that had just been obliterated. The Senetean Army was coming though.

"HOLD LINE! DOWN SPEARS!" the war chiefs yelled at their part of the line. I stood in front of the fifty men under my command and ordered the spears to be lowered. The line consisted of two orders, one with spears and one with swords and shields. The shield line put up their shields and, behind them, were spears protruding out. I was at the front with the swords. "HOLD!" I yelled out along the line.

The other corneals followed my lead and the enemy advanced towards us...

XXIII

The ground shook as the remaining five hundred men marched towards us, slowly but surely. The archers drew their arrows and the sound of bows creaking filled the air. When they were within twenty metres, "FIRE!"

Fifty arrows flew away to their destination, thudding into the first line. People fell but they kept on marching.

"RELOAD!" Fifty hands reached into the pouch of arrows and drew one, fitting it to their bow and drawing back to full capacity.

"FIRE!"

Another fifty arrows flew away. This time more hit their mark, sending twenty men falling to the ground in anguish. Another thirty seconds and they would be upon us.

"FIRE AT WILL!"

Arrows fired at them at every second destroying their third line.

"ARCHERS! FALL BACK!"

The archers fell back to the safety of the steps, giving them the height to snipe of any of the enemy.

"HOLD LINE! STANDBY!"

Then they were upon us.

They flung themselves at us, most of them hitting the wall of spears, but some managing to weave their way through it.

"PUSH FORWARD!"

The spears charged forward, impaling the next line of soldiers.

"DRAW SWORDS!"

The spears were dropped to the floor and the swords were drawn.

"CHARGE!"

I charged into the fray, cutting down people left and right. The archers gave us support from above and many a person fell before I could get to them, with an arrow in their throat. But no matter how many we cut down more kept coming through the gateway. Damn that Mistweaver.

We were, no matter how hard we tried, being pushed back. There were too many of them and our numbers were dwindling. The archers had run out of arrows and we fleeing up the steps and we were being pushed back against them.

I sliced at a young soldier who was locked in

combat with Corneal Laurence. He was forced to duck and I brought my pommel down on his head, not killing but knocking out the attacker.

"Thanks," said Corneal Laurence.

I nodded and turned to look at the gateway.

More soldiers were coming through. Another hundred. We could not hold back against more. We were stretched thin as it was and, if they pierced our line, we would fall.

"FALL BACK TO THE CITY HALL! FALL BACK!"

We ran for the steps. Their muskets shot down many men as we fled to the City Hall, but we kept on going. Finally we reached the strong metal door. I flung myself inside and the door shut behind me with a satisfying thunk.

The remaining fifty men barricaded themselves inside the Hall and then we rested.

"We are TRAPPED! There is no way out of here!" cried a Balbarian corneal.

"He's right. We will die in here no matter how hard we try," admitted the Trilenster war chief.

"Come ON!" I exclaimed. "You're warriors. You live to die and kill. What better opportunity is there for this to be your moment of fame! Yes, we will die. But we can die trying to stop the menace of the Senetean Empire!"

The people around me nodded and they started to

stand up. But there were some who clearly did not agree.

"ARE YOU CRAZY! THEY WILL SLAUGHTER YOU!" yelled the Balbar and Trilenster war chiefs as we strode towards the door.

"I told you before. We're warriors. We live to die." And with that we kicked open the door.

XXIV

The army they had gathered outside was beyond imagining. There must have been thousands. I picked up an axe that was lying on the floor and the last five Icrises soldiers walked down the steps into the cold embrace of death.

I jumped into the fray. And then justice came to the rescue. The five ships that had been sent to rescue civilians had returned, and their guns were blazing!

The cannon balls ripped into the front ranks of the enemy, destroying all sense of order. "CHARGE!" shouted the Icrises war chief. He flung himself at the enemy, cutting two in half has he landed. I followed his lead and swung my axe, cutting down any approaching soldiers. One attacker I cut in half.

The bombardment continued, making large dents in the ground and filling the air with the noise of screaming, as someone was hit directly by a cannon ball and was ripped into hundreds of pieces.

The remaining Senetean army started to escape towards the gate. They failed to predict the next bit of our plan.

The remaining cavalry units charged out of the gate, cutting down the fleeing army. We rode on to the main gate, killing any stragglers. "FOR ICRISES!" the war chief yelled, straight before we charged into the enemy lines.

They did not put up much resistance against us. All that was left were the generals and the cooks and other mundane jobs like that. They swiftly surrendered and we took them back inside the city to be locked up. They certainly deserved it.

Back at the City Hall, the other war chiefs finally got the courage to open the door. They stepped out onto the Overlook and for once they were happy. They had won, after all the doubt and sorrow that they had spread through the ranks. The war chiefs embraced and they smiled.

XXV

The feast at Kakuri was legendary. Foods from all around the world were brought here, just to celebrate the victory and mourn the five thousand men lost. All that remained was fifty odd men, some cavalry, some archers and some soldiers. The civilians were brought back to the city and they were told whether their dear child had survived the battle. In most cases, they had not.

A mass grave was made a little way from the city and a funeral was held for the dead. Some bodies we could not even find. Or some were so mangled that we could not recognise who it was. Needless to say, these families were the most upset.

Corneals from all the clans had come to celebrate the war that we had won. The war chiefs sat at the top of the table with the corneals sitting on either side. It was the first time all clans had been together in a feast like this, so there was much drinking and singing.

Bards were brought from each land to sing and rejoice for the victory we had won and it also added a genial atmosphere. Then, the sound of metal against glass and all was silent. It was time for the war chief to make his speech.

"Many lives have been lost in these past days and weeks," he said. "Either through being slaughtered by the Senetean Army, or fighting for his country, or both. And I tell you now, those men and women, have more right than me to be the war chief." This was unexpected. People looked up.

"They died with honour. And nothing can stop us from doing that. We have also fought side by side with the other factions. And no matter how many wars we may have fought with each other, we put aside our differences and fought against the tyranny of the Senetean Army. Now the Senetean Army is defeated and the lands of Senetea are open for the taking. Shall this result in another war or shall we share up the bounties of that land?"

There was complete silence as we waited for his answer. "Let no more young blood be spilled for the petty want of mortals. Let us strike an alliance, so we can live in peace and harmony!" he yelled out across the table.

Then the cheering begun, though there were some who did not join in and held a look of disgust on their faces. "I propose a toast," said the war chief. "Long live the Barbarian Alliance!"

THE END

www.ingramcontent.com/pod-product-compliance
Lightning Source LLC
Chambersburg PA
CBHW030555130626
46552CB00006B/2560